人物介绍

　　我是可爱的小·猪佩奇。我来自英国，今年四岁了。我和弟弟乔治、猪爸爸、猪妈妈一起住在山顶小·屋。我爱我的爸爸、妈妈还有弟弟。我喜欢和我最好的朋友小·羊苏茜一起玩，我喜欢去拜访猪爷爷、猪奶奶，我还喜欢照顾我弟弟乔治。但是，我最喜欢的事情是蹦泥坑，大声地笑，大声地猪哼哼。

　　等你和我做了好朋友，你就会发现，我和你很像或者是和你身边的朋友很像。同时，我还是小·朋友学习英语的好伙伴。

　　今年，《小·猪佩奇》动画片也将来到中国，为中国小·朋友带来笑声和欢乐。

天气晴朗。小猪佩奇和小羊苏茜在打网球。

"接球，苏茜！"佩奇一边击球，一边叫。

现在轮到苏茜了。

"接球，佩奇！"苏茜叫。球从佩奇的头上飞了过去。哦，天哪！

"哇——"乔治感觉有点被冷落。

"乔治，对不起。"佩奇说，"我们不能带你一起玩，因为我们只有两个球拍。"

"乔治可以当球童。"苏茜说。

"乔治，球童可是很重要的工作哟。"佩奇说。

佩奇和苏茜玩得很高兴，虽然她们经常接不到球。

"球童！"她们一起喊。

"哼哧，哼哧！"乔治不太高兴，因为他一直跑来跑去捡球，非常累。

佩奇的朋友们来了。"大家好。"佩奇说，"我们在打网球呢。"

　　"我们可以一起玩吗？"小狗丹尼问。

　　"我们的球拍不够呀。"苏茜回答说。

"那我们来踢足球吧。"丹尼说。

"足球！好棒！"大家一起欢呼。

"我们可以分组对抗，男生一队，女生一队。"佩奇说。

"每个队都需要一名守门员。"丹尼说。

"我，我！"小马佩德罗说。

"我，我！"小兔瑞贝卡说。

于是，佩德罗和瑞贝卡当守门员。

"男生队要开球了。"丹尼说。

小兔理查德得到了球，他带球快跑，躲过了佩奇、苏茜和小猫卡迪，直奔球门而去。

理查德射门，球从瑞贝卡的身边飞过，落进球门里。"得分！"丹尼和佩德罗一起叫。

"男生队赢了！"丹尼欢呼。

"不公平！我们还没有准备好。"佩奇抱怨道。

18

瑞贝卡捡起球，开始跑。

"嘿！"丹尼叫道，"犯规！你不能用手拿球。"

"我能！"瑞贝卡说，"因为我是守门员。"

瑞贝卡把球扔进球门，球恰好从佩德罗身边飞过。

"得分！"瑞贝卡叫道。

“这个球不算。”佩德罗说。

“算。”佩奇说。

“不算，不算！”丹尼咆哮着。

“真吵啊！”猪爸爸说，
“我来当裁判。从现在开始，
哪个队先进球哪个队赢。”

就在大家还站在那儿讨论的时候，理查德和乔治已经带着球跑了。

"球呢？"佩奇问。

但是已经晚了。理查德越过佩德罗，直接把球踢进了球门里。

"好棒！男生队赢了！"丹尼欢呼。

"足球是一个很蠢的游戏。"佩奇失望地说。

"等一等。"猪爸爸说，"男孩们把球踢进了自己的大门里。这就是说：女生队赢了。"

"真的吗？"女孩们欢呼，"好棒！"

"足球是一个伟大的游戏！"佩奇开心地说。

"哈哈哈！"大家都笑了。

It's a sunny day and Peppa Pig and Suzy Sheep are playing tennis.

"To you, Suzy!" cheers Peppa, hitting the ball.

Now, it's Suzy's turn.

"To you, Peppa!" she cries, hitting the ball straight over Peppa's head. Oh dear!

"Waaaa!" George feels a bit left out.

"Sorry, George," says Peppa. "You can't play tennis. We only have two racquets."

"George can be the ball boy!" cheers Suzy.

"Being a ball boy is a very important job, George," says Peppa.

Peppa and Suzy are having lots of fun, but they keep missing the ball.
"Ball boy!" they shout together.
"Huff, puff!" George is not having fun. He keeps running to get the ball and he is very tired!

"Hello, everyone," cries Peppa when her friends arrive. "We're playing tennis."
"Can we play too?" asks Danny Dog.
"There aren't enough racquets," replies Suzy Sheep.

第 11 面

"Let's play football then," says Danny Dog.
"Football! Hooray!" everyone cheers.

第 12 面

"We can play girls against boys," says Peppa.
"Each team needs a goalkeeper," says Danny Dog.
"Me, me!" shouts Pedro Pony.
"Me, me!" cries Rebecca Rabbit.

第 14 面

Pedro Pony and Rebecca Rabbit decide to be the goalkeepers.
"The boys' team will start!" says Danny Dog.
Richard Rabbit gets the ball and runs very fast, right by Peppa Pig, Suzy Sheep and Candy Cat and straight up to the . . .

第 16 面

. . . "GOAL!" cry Danny and Pedro together, as Richard Rabbit kicks the ball straight past Rebecca Rabbit and into the net.
"The boy is a winner!" cheers Danny Dog.
"That's not fair, we weren't ready, " moans Peppa.

第 19 面

Rebecca Rabbit picks up the ball and runs.
"Hey!" shouts Danny Dog. "That's cheating! You can't hold the ball."
"Yes I can!" says Rebecca, "I'm the goalkeeper."
Rebecca throws the ball into the goal, straight past Pedro Pony.
"GOAL!" she cries.

第 20 面

"That goal is not allowed," says Pedro.
"Yes, it is," says Peppa.
"No, it isn't!" barks Danny.
"What a lot of noise," snorts Daddy Pig.
"I'll be the referee. The next team to get a goal will win the game."

第 23 面

Richard Rabbit and George run off with the football, while everyone is still talking.
"Where's the ball?" asks Peppa.
But it's too late! Richard Rabbit kicks the ball straight into the goal, past Pedro Pony.
"Hooray! The boys win!" cries Danny.

"Football is a silly game," sighs Peppa, disappointed.

"Just a moment," says Daddy Pig. "The boys scored in their own goal, that means the girls win!"

"Really?" gasp all the girls. "Hooray!"

"Football is a great game!" cheers Peppa.

"Ha ha ha!" everyone laughs.

看完了这本图画书，让我们来学习几个与运动相关的
单词和句子吧。

football 足球

tennis 网球

goalkeeper 守门员

goal 进球

Let's play football.
我们来踢足球吧。

Football is a great game.
足球是一个伟大的游戏。